D1617316

Look Busy

One hundred 100-word stories
by and for the easily distracted

● ◐ ◑ ◯ ◯ ◯ ◑ ◐

by Jane McDermott

In Memory of Michael Rubin, Fourteen Hills Press annually publishes a student work of exceptional accomplishment. Each book is selected through an open competition by an independent judge. Funding is provided by the students of SFSU through the Instructionally Related Activities Fund.

The 2014 Michael Rubin Book Award was judged by Jacob M. Appel.

Disclaimer
These stories are works of fiction. Names, characters, places and incidents are either products of the author's imagination or are used factiously, and any resemblance to actual persons, living or dead, events, or locales is entirely coincidental.

Cover art by Cathy Ryan, cathyryanprints.com.
Cover designed by Paula Guidugli.

Set in Cochin.

ISBN: 978-1-889292-64-9

Printed in the United States of America.

Look Busy

One hundred 100-word stories
by and for the easily distracted

by Jane McDermott

Winner of the 2014 Michael Rubin Book Award
Fourteen Hills : San Francisco

*f*or all the odd girls

One

All bees know what they're supposed to be doing and do what they're supposed to do. They work tirelessly and in unison for the benefit of the hive, not themselves. In their lifetime they work all aspects of the hive and produce a great product. Their lives are short, just six weeks, but they work in service to the hive until their wings are frayed. Unless they die from disease or misadventure, they return to the hive to die. After they are dead, their bee sisters sweep them out of the hive and go back to work.

Bees are crazy.

Two

"For the love of God, woman, open this door!"

A few times a month, the pounding and pleading sometimes went on for nearly an hour. My mother would quietly but firmly talk to him through the closed door as he shouted and begged.

"Open the door, missus! Please, open up!" he'd cry.

"Mr. Sullivan," she'd say over and over. "Go home. This is not your house. You live down the road. Go home."

Sometimes the police would come, but usually my mother would manage to convince him of his error and, sobbing, he'd go try his luck at another door.

Three

When you must replace someone at work with someone else, the expectation is that the new person will be better than the one replaced. Time goes by and it may seem that you have accomplished what you set out to do: replace someone with someone better. More time goes by and you realize that the new person isn't really any better; the new person is just different than the original person. Nothing has improved; everything's just different.

Sometimes different can pass for better, but eventually you realize that nothing has been gained and you now have another person to replace.

O

Four

My mother's roommate at the nursing home, Grace, slept soundly through my mother's death and the ensuing activity and people in the room.

In the morning, with my mother gone Grace would have perhaps pondered whether she had ever had a roommate. In a few days, someone else would be installed in the second bed.

It didn't matter to Grace when my mother was there; it didn't matter to her when she was gone. By then, Grace was used to people disappearing. That's the way it was.

What mattered to Grace was if anyone had dibs on my mother's TV.

○

Five

The Lord works in mysterious ways and she figured He'd outdone Himself this time when she saw her front lawn strewn in auto parts. She was almost blinded by all the chrome. She'd yet to see the cause of it all: a jack-knifed semi planted in the gully at the end of her property, its rear doors open, cargo gone, and driver's face splayed on the windshield.

"The Lord wants me to shine my light," she thought. "Go out into the world and shine, shine, shine."

(She no longer had a friend in Jesus, but she didn't know that yet.)

O

Six

Winter lasts like sixteen months in England. It makes you want to kill yourself. England is one giant runny nose in winter — inside and out — a gray, wet, shivering misery.

I lived there in the seventies. Now the English have gone all European and modern and run around with cell phones and have double-hung windows and refrigeration worth a damn.

But when I lived there I was shoving coins into a bullshit box on the wall to make the lights run so don't get all "Rule, Britannia!" on me.

Their winters still suck. And beans on toast is an abomination.

Seven

He seemed endearing at first. He was winsome and obliging without being ingratiating. It seemed that he understood his job was something that she'd written and intended for herself. He deferred to her and accepted her counsel. He was gracious and so, too, was she.

But after a while she realized he had no idea of what had happened. What she thought was deference to her situation was actually distraction. He was self-absorbed, complacent, and had no idea of his effect on her.

It wasn't insensitivity; he was simply unaware. Clueless.

Oblivion looks a lot like diplomacy at first glance.

Eight

Out for a walk on a cloudless Saturday morning, I wandered into a yard sale. The yard was strewn with household goods and garden tools — the detritus of domestic life.

Shielded from the sun, a red-haired woman was thumbing through a magazine while a red-haired baby chewed her way through a copy of *Our Bodies, Ourselves*.

"How much for the kid?" I asked.

She squinted up at me. "Make me an offer," she said. "I've got two more in the back yard. I'll give you a good deal on the set."

And that's how Maureen Flaherty and I became friends.

Nine

A woman sets food-laden platters in front of her eagerly awaiting children. As her children hand her their plates, she is filled with a sense of uneasiness.

She hands back their portions and serves herself when it suddenly occurs to her that these are not children at all, but cats dressed in children's clothing.

The cats eat happily and with gusto while the woman watches them carefully.

Finally, she says: "You're not children, are you."

"No," the cats reluctantly admit.

The woman nods sadly and makes a mental note to bring this up with their father when he comes home.

Ten

While at a restaurant, we saw whom we thought was a friend of ours sidling up to the bar with someone who wasn't her partner.

We weren't sure it was her, but while we were trying to catch a glimpse we discussed the ramifications of a positive ID. Suppose it was her, suppose she was cheating on her partner, what would we do? And if our friends were to break up over this tryst, whose friend would this cheater become? Would we remain friends with both? Oh, the awkwardness of not knowing whom to invite to parties.

It wasn't her.

Eleven

In Paris, I sat under a Buvez Pepsi sign separating French francs from Swiss francs. After several days without speaking English, my head ached over the constant internal translating just to get myself fed and around town. Suddenly, I became aware of English being spoken, Irish-accented English. I strained to locate where the voice was coming from, but I couldn't tell.

I almost cried.

It was February, cold and rainy. I was exhausted from negotiating everything by myself. Paris — beautiful, bewildering — pretty much sucked.

However, the next visit, also in February, was great.

Euros helped. Not being alone — even better.

O

Twelve

Before our friend killed herself there were no warning signs as far as we could tell. After the fact we realized that there had been plenty. None of us interpreted her peculiarities as suicidal or a cry for help. We thought she was a little kooky—that's all. Maybe giving away all her stuff should have been a clue, but none of us realized how miserable or desperate she had become.

Well, now we know and of course we all feel terrible about it. The next time one of our friends starts acting strangely, we'll be on top of it.

○

Thirteen

I loved swinging, but I hated the jumping off part — a peer requirement.

It's not the same since that time we all dared each other to get higher then jump off.

I did alright, but Jimmy was masterful — he practically spun all the way around.

That hot, airless day he pumped like mad. He jumped off twenty feet in the air. He landed like a gymnast and stood with his arms raised. Then the swing hit him in the head, knocking him out cold. An ambulance came and he was driven off, a bloody mess.

He died later that night.

O

Fourteen

He colors his hair red because he thinks it makes him looks younger. What it does instead is make him look like what he really is: an aging, silly, sad, insecure, desperate, gay man who is trying to not be overlooked in favor of a younger person with greater confidence and better skills. His innate flamboyance used to be magical. He was the smart, pretty one without even trying. Now, he knows he is overcompensating and fooling no one, but he just can't stop himself.

It's funny how things can become more obvious the more we try to hide them.

Fifteen

His bookshelves were loaded with travel books and unreadable European fiction. Ethnic art was strewn about his apartment. He knew a few languages and read constantly about foreign places and although he had never left the country, he considered himself a world citizen. In fact, he seldom left town. He felt sheepish about this and never mentioned it to anyone. However, whenever he heard stories of lost luggage, illness while traveling, not to mention theft, he felt confident that staying put was prudent.

Besides, in the end, he believed, it doesn't matter where you've been; it matters what you've bought.

Sixteen

I saw my neighbors naked last night. We share a fence. They bought the house catty-corner behind us. It used to be a sweet eight-hundred-square-foot bungalow, but they turned it into a three-tiered craftsman wedding cake nightmare. They've covered their backyard with fake grass and have a gigantic hot tub that takes up half the yard. They're seldom there.

But last night I saw them from my bedroom window as they came outside, slipped off their towels, stood for a moment, and immerged into their hot tub.

They're young and in good shape, but otherwise nothing special.

Seventeen

While in a café I watched a kid with a nose ring and a dripping, miserable cold sit forlornly over a cup of herbal tea. Periodically, he'd gingerly blow his enflamed, punctured nose and dab at his red swollen nostrils. He was the picture of suffering.

I felt very sorry for him while at the same time wondered why he didn't just take the damn nose ring out until his cold got better.

And then I remembered all the foolish things I've done in the name of coolness, smiled, and was grateful. Oh, to be young again? Thank you, no.

Eighteen

I like to swear loudly at people when I'm driving by myself in the car. You'd think that doing this might be exhausting, but it's truly exhilarating. Try it. Don't worry about looking stupid—people will think that you're singing along to the radio or talking on your cell.

You don't have to drive very long or far before someone does something stupid or annoying. If they don't, you can pick people driving cars that you find irritating or have ugly children—you get to choose!

For your own safety, remember to keep the windows rolled up when doing this.

◐

Nineteen

Pale, plump, and bunny-eyed, with a curious patch of black hair on the back of their heads, the albino siblings would always waddle into Mass together. There were four of them and they looked stunningly alike. They were ultra-white children in a transcendently white community. Having translucent skin is not uncommon in the Irish, but theirs was otherworldly. It was the black patch in a field of snow-white hair that you tended to notice first. People would remark on the odd patches of black hair, completely missing the point of how bizarre in general these children were.

I envied them.

O

Twenty

A woman awoke to find a bugle in the middle of her forehead. She lay in bed half the morning worried sick over how this would affect her dating prospects.

Eventually, she got up and dealt with an even graver concern—getting dressed. She opted for sweats. Her gold flats and triangular gold earrings—both usually much too dressy for sweats—were perfect. "The ability to accessorize is what separates us from wild animals," she reasoned. This was nothing more than a fashion challenge and challenge, history shows us, is the handmaiden of opportunity.

Neurosis is not without its rewards.

○

Twenty-One

I had a pixie haircut as a kid. My mother would often trim my bangs. She had trouble cutting them evenly so she just made them shorter until sometimes I was left with no bangs at all. On Sundays, my scratchy petticoat caused my dress to stick way out. The dress prevented me from putting my arms down completely by my side. I also wore slippery dress shoes that caused me to alter my walk. So between the shoes, the bangs, and the dress, I kind of looked like a chimp in drag going to church. Felt like one, too.

O

Twenty-Two

Having succeeded in duping management into believing that his self-aggrandizing posturing was leadership, he was given increasing responsibility for a number of projects.

His subordinates loathed him, which galvanized their resolve to devise subtle ways to subvert his directives and thwart progress.

He explained to management that it was staff's fault that projects were off-target, but even as he said this he realized that the fault was, in fact, his and he understood suddenly that the reason he had risen in the ranks was to own all the blame.

"Damn—I can take that straight to the bank," he thought.

Twenty-Three

In downtown Berkeley, you often don't hear the high-pitched whine of the electric wheelchair careening down the sidewalk until a millisecond before you need to get out of its way. By the time it is upon you, the sound is more like an insistent mosquito searching for blood in the middle of the night.

Dodging out of the way, you might mumble an obscenity. You might also make eye contact with the driver. Her eyes say what she cannot: "No, I can't control this thing any more than you could if you could move only two fingers, you able-bodied asshole."

Twenty-Four

I learned to mix drinks when I was still wearing pajamas with feet. Seven and Seven. CC and soda. Easy stuff to make. People called them "Susie's Ten Fingers" because I needed both hands to carry the glass, that's how young I was.

I learned to drink at thirteen. Boone's Farm. Strawberry Hill. Occasionally, Mogen David. I drank straight from the bottle taking big gulps with closed eyes. I'd swallow and hope for the best. Many of my friends would get sick; I rarely did.

How you hold your liquor changes over time and changes you.

I know that now.

Twenty-Five

I got a sewing machine for my fourteenth birthday. "Wow," I remember thinking, "who's this for?"

I appreciated it as a beautiful piece of equipment, but all I ever managed to make with it was drawstring gym bags.

I think my mother had visions of us looking through pattern books together. We'd research buttonhole attachments and—*surprise!*—a buttonholer would be under the tree for me on Christmas! She'd help me pin the hem of my prom dress. Oh, the fun we'd have selecting fabric and strolling through the notions looking for the perfect trim and perfect buttons!

Sorry Mom.

Twenty-Six

My school building was a million years old. Its cast iron stairs let me see up girls' skirts. Although I was a girl myself, this was something I liked to do. On a bathroom break during my study halls I'd peer into classrooms and find a girl I liked to look at.

The one who still stays in my mind had red hair and skin so white—the only kind of skin you can have when your hair is red.

But, oh, one day up close I saw she had brown eyes she had brown eyes she had brown eyes.

Twenty-Seven

For months the session before mine was a blind couple. I'd wait in my car for them to come out so I could watch them. Watching people without them knowing is a guilty pleasure of mine, but as the couple was blind I didn't have to hide what I was doing.

Usually, they would come out, harness their dogs, and walk off. But one time they came out and stood and talked. Then the blind man goosed the blind woman. She jumped up, startled, and they both stepped on their dogs. The dogs started yelping and barking.

It was hilarious.

O

Twenty-Eight

Quitting a job you've had for years might be a sweet experience. People might take you to lunch. There might be a poignant farewell party and a cake with your name on it. You might get an engraved Lucite clock with some commemorative words. The words wouldn't be clever—they would need you to write them in order for them to be clever and it's your Lucite clock for Pete's sake.

Or, you might end up with the HR assistant handing you your last check on your way out, twenty-seven packets of soy sauce from your desk in your purse.

○

Twenty-Nine

My father was one of the unsung heroes of WWII. When the drill instructor barked, "Any of you mugs know how to type?" my father was able to quickly compute that *type* = *desk* = *safety* and raised his hand. Although he could type with only one finger on each hand, it proved to be plenty for the reams of forms Uncle Sam had him fill in. His involvement in the war was an unheralded, but critical paper trail that began in 1941 in North Africa and ended in 1945 around Florence.

My dad: making the world safe for bureaucracy.

O

Thirty

I'm dating a woman whose son calls himself Spit. He's in a band called DNR. She seemed terrific at first. Slowly though — and mothers can't help it — it became obvious how preoccupied she is with him.

The kid looks like an extra from a slasher movie, but he's ok. He has that scared, sweet, sullen thing going on that is the hallmark of being sixteen.

It's strange to be dating someone who has a kid the age I was when I started dating. It makes me realize that my criteria haven't changed — still looking for danger, Mom, and unconditional love.

Thirty-One

I met a homeless panhandler in San Francisco. She was wearing leopard print leggings, a Giants' cap, a hot pink leotard, and a button that said, "Today I'm Irish."

She asked me first for $3.77 and then for $2.89. How could I refuse? I didn't have exact change and ended up giving her four bucks.

She thanked me profusely and said, "You know, I don't care that you're gay. I'm totally fine with that."

"How do you know I'm gay?" I asked her.

"Dude," she replied looking at me like I'm from another planet. "How do you know I'm homeless?"

Thirty-Two

In high school when a boy asked me out, I knew the evening would end with me fending him off like a wild animal.

Then I met Frank. He asked permission to kiss me rather than just pressing his lips against mine, jamming his tongue down my throat, and poking all his bumpy parts against me. Frank told me he wanted to kiss me and then asked if he could. When I said yes, he kissed me like he was tasting chocolate, like I was a taste he'd been looking for his whole life.

He scared me half to death.

Thirty-Three

Two children were busily digging a hole in a park. A man walking by came over and asked them, "Digging to China?"

The children did not stop or look up, but continued with their feverish digging.

The man stood and watched them for a while and then said, "Are you digging to China?"

The children stopped digging and looked up at the man. Standing waist deep in their hole, one said, "No, not China," and the other said, "Hell."

The man clasped his hand over his mouth and ran from them in horror.

"China," they sighed and grimly continued digging.

Thirty-Four

A big reason why lousy employees don't do any work is because they are too busy figuring out ways to get out of their assignments. Of course, the less productive they become, the less work that is assigned to them. Therefore, over time, they must devise truly ingenious ways to goof off.

Beware of any disciplinary action you might take as it can easily be thwarted by their charge that you never made the assignment clear or some such bullshit. In other words, you are a bad manager and it is your fault they suck.

Incompetence is a full-time job.

Thirty-Five

"Is Helen Hunt a lesbian?" I key in.

Now I wait for an answer.

Some people would call this crazy; it's no more crazy than explaining to my mother that I'm not a telemarketer, I've never been a telemarketer. I'm in marketing. *Mar-ket-ing.* It's so much easier when she doesn't ask me questions, my mother. It's so much easier when she just talks and talks. It keeps me from having to explain myself. It's easier being misunderstood when you're not trying to explain.

I've got an accordion strapped on. I'm wearing a keyboard while using a keyboard.

Is this multi-tasking?

O

Thirty-Six

You are writing and wanting to change all the names so that you can honestly say it's fiction except that changing the names makes everything sound wrong and you're trying so hard to be authentic what with all the therapy. So then you change the names back but you add some stuff that didn't happen and invent some characters so that it really is fiction. Now it feels authentic with real names, but it's fiction because you've added some stuff that didn't happen and made up some people.

No one will know or care how tortuous this is for you.

○

Thirty-Seven

It might be my imagination, but my mother seems to attract catastrophe. Disaster seems to be steps away from her at all times. It could be her aura, or her karma. Or maybe just her mouth and how she chooses to use it. It's a dangerous weapon; it should require a license.

I went into the house and told my partner, "You're going to have to go out and fasten my mother's seat belt for her. I'm afraid if I get that close to her I won't be able to resist the urge to strangle her."

I'm all about safety.

O

Thirty-Eight

I'm not a lawyer although I work with lawyers. I'm very good at what I do and have over twenty-five years' experience doing it, but hardly a day goes by when the lawyers with whom I work don't find some way to remind me that I'm not a lawyer.

It's not because they're mean—although many of them are very mean—or because they're stupid or insensitive—although many of them are those things, too. It's because they are lawyers and lawyers are "like that."

It is like working with forty alcoholics who use their condition to justify being assholes.

Thirty-Nine

In the steam room, I looked through the mist as the woman lying on the bench across from me stretched extravagantly and luxuriously like a cat. Then she farted; a loud, staccato, wet-sounding fart. I imagined bubbles percolating up from her butt as she stood in the pool.

She continued to fart. And not dainty little boops, but ripping, deliberate farts all the louder from the echoing acoustics in the tiled steam room.

In the shower, she made brief but certain eye contact with me as if to say, "You didn't hear anything. I don't know what you're talking about."

Forty

My mother would sometimes get all gung ho about making plans for us to do something as a family until it dawned on her that we would be the family she'd have to do it with and then she'd get all angry and huffy as she rushed around grabbing snacks and sweaters for everyone while bellowing at us to get in the car, damn it, and then screeching out the driveway, slamming into drive, leaving a little rubber, and careening us off to some activity, my little sister crying and my brother's eyes wide with fear.

Good times, good times.

Forty-One

We experience emotions that are beyond our ability to express because of the limitations of language, not the lack of depth to our feelings or an indication we are numb or are not feeling anything. Words are often woefully inadequate to describe our inner landscape in which we can experience emotional material that is elusive and confluent. Additionally, as everyone experiences emotions in different ways no response can be deemed more valid than another. We are all unique.

So shut the fuck up about my deadened soul, my under-developed emotional "quotient," and my unwillingness to communicate.

You're pissing me off.

Forty-Two

Cheryl Bailey had cooties. Everyone knew this. She had many siblings, the family had no money, and her mother had only one arm. No one was sure how or if any of these facts contributed to Cheryl's cootiness, but we were certain that they must have somehow.

Once, we were learning a square dance and everyone quickly paired up. I was left with Cheryl. She wouldn't even make eye contact. When the music began I reluctantly took her hand and it was remarkably smooth and soft. It was a lovely hand. It felt like it had never been held before.

Forty-Three

A woman from the Chinese restaurant down the street goes through our trash stealing our recyclables. I pretend that I don't see or hear her although I do and it pisses me off that she does what she does. It feels like an invasion of privacy.

She pretends she doesn't see me either although she might. Then again, she might not. She probably doesn't care one way or the other. She might be horrified that I'm just throwing these things away and is setting a good example for me: "White people. You have to show them how to do everything."

O

Forty-Four

I have made neurosis the cornerstone of my work. I have often thought of writing about people who are well-adjusted and happy but, frankly, I simply do not have the energy or the talent to write that type of fiction. It would be too much of a stretch. I am exhausted just thinking about it.

So, instead, I write about what I know—like all the experts say to do. I write about lumpy, sad, nervous, disorganized, irritable, yet witty people.

Actually, I don't do that at all—I write about whatever comes out. It's the best I can do.

○

Forty-Five

I hum.

It's constant, apparently. It's very soft and barely audible, but audible enough so that most people
can hear it. It's like white noise, I've been told—
like a refrigerator hum or the high frequency whine
of fluorescent lights. Sometimes it's more like a *grr*
sound, like a steady clearing of the throat. I make
the *grr* sound more when I'm working and busy
than, say, when I'm just hanging out. My humming
is an endearing idiosyncrasy and an annoying tic
in equal measure. I think of it as a way of knowing
that I'm on and operable.

Sorry.

◯

Forty-Six

If I stepped in front of a fast train, if I hurled myself from the top of a tall building, if I shot myself in the head, if I swam out into the ocean as far as I could until I got tired and drowned, if I took poison, if I deliberately drove my car very fast into a wall, if I jumped off a bridge into a very deep body of water, if I took a fistful of pills and chased it down with a fifth of vodka, if I slit my wrists, then *then* what would I do?

Forty-Seven

Drinking is integral to my ancestral culture. I am not sure what effect ethnicity has actually had; we could be Finnish and drink a lot assuming that temperament and circumstance remained the same. Considering some of the alternative bad habits—I'm sure there are some—drinking can seem almost charming. Ugly scenes, broken promises, and alienated children notwithstanding. We all know it leads to ruin, but when the banshee boozer gene kicks in, it's hard to stop.

And yes, the irony is not lost on me that the place I bring my empty bottles to is called a redemption center.

Forty-Eight

While driving from San Francisco to LA with his elderly mother, three-year-old daughter, pregnant wife, and a dog, he could not travel for more than about forty-five minutes before someone had to pee or puke.

As they made Conestoga wagon-like progress heading south he imagined that back in the old days, you just did what you needed to do and then caught up with the wagon train. There was none of this pulling over nonsense—no rest stops, no vending machines.

"There might have been beef jerky, though," he thought as he gnawed through the twelfth piece of the day.

Forty-Nine

Sometimes someone will tell me that his old college roommate was gay. He'll tell me that he was impressed that although his roommate was gay he never "tried" anything with him. As if "homosexual" and "rapist" were synonymous. As if anyone, gay or straight, given half a chance would do him. As if his moronic revelations are somehow supposed to make me feel safe and accepted in the world.

When told stories like this I nod and say something inane like, "Well, there you go." I sigh inside while feeling another crack develop in my infrastructure.

It never gets easier.

Fifty

In the crazy yoga class it is fifteen hundred degrees and everyone acts like nothing's going on. Everyone moves through yoga postures glistening like they've been dipped in Vaseline because it's fifteen hundred degrees in the room, but no one lets on that it's out of the ordinary.

When the class is small, the teacher gives instruction and walks around helping students make adjustments. When she came to help me as I struggled with a posture she asked me if I had any injuries.

"Well," I said. "I had a really difficult childhood."

"Remember to breathe," she offered. "Keep breathing."

Fifty-One

I dreamt that Bob Levine cut my hair. He had made a very compelling argument that cutting it was "the way to go" so I reluctantly agreed.

I had asked him—and continued to ask him while he cut—if he was absolutely sure about this. My hair had taken a long time to grow out and a new hairstyle was part of my ongoing quest for tangible change.

He nodded and cut very close to my head. The scissors sounded like hedge clippers in my ears.

All he kept saying was, "Yes, yes. This is what we must do."

O

Fifty-Two

When the new Mass came about, many people were upset. English just didn't have the same cachet as Latin and it was unnerving having the priest facing us as we watched his every slurp, wipe, and chew.

The sign of peace was particularly anxiety producing as no one seemed to know just what the pope had in mind for us to do.

I was hoping for an actual sign—like instructing a runner to steal first or giving the thumbs up.

A handshake? Really? You'd think the people who gave us the genuflect, feet kissing, and ashes could do better.

○

Fifty-Three

I almost died being born and my mother almost died giving birth to me. My father celebrated not losing us both by going out, getting drunk, and then wrapping a car around a tree, dying instantly.

Because it was a borrowed car and my father wasn't carrying a wallet, it took almost two days for the police to notify my mother of his death. By that time, weak from a hard delivery, she was nearly crazed with worry. She had to be sedated when she got the news and stopped nursing me.

She recovered in body, but never in mind.

O

Fifty-Four

The teenaged son of the woman I'm dating plays guitar and sings. He's not bad. One evening he gave us a strum and a tune.

"Hey dude," he began.

"Hey Jude," I interrupted.

"What?" he said.

"It's 'Hey Jude,'" I said. "Not 'Hey dude.' Jude."

"Dude, Jude," the kid said. "BFD."

"Yeah, honey," my girlfriend said. "What difference does it make? I think 'Dude' is kind of cute. Why do you always have to be so critical?"

"Yeah, chill out, *Jude*," said the son, and mother and son laughed together and looked at each other adoringly.

I hated them both.

Fifty-Five

It was as if he was being bathed in a warm and healing light. His entire being was washed with a vibrancy and virility that he hadn't felt in years and yet he was completely calm and relaxed. He had a sense of being near gentle water with a soft moist breeze caressing him. He couldn't remember ever feeling so truly liberated and with such a profound sense of well-being.

Slowly he opened his eyes and awoke. He was naked and lying on his back. The puppy was asleep between his legs with its mouth wrapped loosely around his penis.

Fifty-Six

When Up With People performed at my public school, we sat bemused through their mercilessly cheerful signature song, "Up With People," grateful to not be in algebra. But after "What Color is God's Skin?" we grew wary. Their thinly veiled Christian perkiness rankled our dour urban edginess. They started to get preachy. And a little creepy.

UWP was an ideological ambush. In fact, we were constantly being told what to do; we didn't need to have God getting all up in our faces. At school.

When church and state separated it really was in the best interests of the children.

Fifty-Seven

My demons are many and robust requiring big, energetic projects to keep them at bay. Like painting my house, for instance.

While painting said house a feckless neighbor asked me if I liked the color.

"Yes, I do," I said politely. This was a learned response. Because the world is full of nosey, rude, and ignorant people who ask inane questions I must maintain civility during their fatuous banter and not stoop to their level. Thus, I said, "Yes, I like it," not, "Do you really think I'd kill myself painting my house a color I hated?"

Deep cleansing breath.

Fifty-Eight

My mother was aware of me more than I realized although not out of her innate maternal concern. It was because I was so *obvious*. At ten, I was already five and a half feet tall, squeezing out of my clothes like the Incredible Hulk with the beginning of bumps that would soon become acne and breasts.

Her way of looking at me seemed to say, "What have you done with my daughter? Where is my little girl?"

Every time I yet again brought up the rear of a line of children my age, I wondered the same thing myself.

Fifty-Nine

My grandmother's hands smelled like lilac. She would clap her hands when she saw me and reach for me and pull me close. "Go get my pocketbook," she'd whisper and I'd run off and retrieve her bag.

She'd open her pocketbook and the lilac smell would intensify—her handkerchief, her plastic rain bonnet, her rosary beads, her roll of Lifesavers, the little envelope that held her coupons, and her wallet all smelled of lilac. "Here," she'd say as she pressed into my hand a dollar which smelled like her wallet, which smelled like her pocketbook, which smelled like her hand.

O

Sixty

When you are out running, you always have the option to stop running, but you never have the option to stop going. You must always finish your run even if it is on your hands and knees. Even when you feel as though you have had enough—you have managed to injure yourself or you are suddenly sick or it is just too damn hot or cold or wet—you still have to get back home and your own locomotion must get you there.

Abrasions and blisters, bowel and bladder emergencies—what do I miss about running?

Everything, dammit, everything.

Sixty-One

On hot summer evenings when I had all the windows open, I prayed that some passerby wouldn't hear my girls screaming, "Stop mommy! No, don't do that! Owie, owie! Help!" and call the police.

I would tell my neighbors if I ever saw them that I was only trying to wash my children's hair. Nothing untoward was going on. They were welcome to come and watch if they didn't believe me. I was even tempted to post a sign on our front door.

My girls carried on so! I'd have shaved their little heads if that wasn't considered child abuse.

O

Sixty-Two

When you are broke, that's the time for a girl to look pretty and sit up straight at the bar. Looking like poverty is a sure way to run into it.

Look like money and your chances for a good dinner, maybe even a good time, improve. There's no sense advertising your misery; misery already gets plenty of business.

I've never had much—chances are you won't either coming from these people and here. But mark my words, if you don't shake off whatever's trying to stick to you it'll become a permanent coat of neediness.

Fortune favors the brave.

Sixty-Three

My relationship with my mother went wrong somewhere in the second trimester. By the time I was born, we had developed a deep and abiding mistrust of each other. In my case, it was over whether she could ever care for me. For her, I eventually realized, it was also over whether she could ever care for me.

Care is relative.

The care a child requires is often different than the care a child receives. For some children, this is a tragedy. For others, who will spend the rest of their lives forgetting that they once were children, it's not.

Sixty-Four

I read a lot of books about quirky English families. There'd be a parcel of kids led by an imaginative older sister. The parents never seemed to notice that a man in a turban was at the dinner table or that the kids had all gone missing or that a zebra was living in the pantry. How cool is that? My mother was able to tell by looking at me that I had smoked a cigarette hours before, although she did not know that my alcoholic father kept chocolate and pornography under the front seat of his car.

I did.

Sixty-Five

Chickens have two modes: on and off.

When they are on, they are cackling, scratching, dust-wallowing, funny, pooping, squabbling, molting, pecking, egg machines. When they are off, they are dead.

On, they are busy, waddling, flapping, squawking, curious, bug eaters. Off, they are dead.

On: greedy, preening. Off: dead.

Their eyes have very few rods; chickens are essentially blind at night. However, their remarkable number of cones allows them to see more acutely than most other creatures in the light. Humans have more rods than cones. However, our lack of humanity and responsibility makes us essentially blind all the time.

Sixty-Six

When she was in the final stages of her illness, with her body debilitated and no position comfortable, she would beg for God to end her misery and let her die. Her family assumed it was the pain talking and began an aggressive regime of pain management. In less than a day, her pain was under control and she was resting comfortably. However, she continued to beg for death, which deeply troubled her husband. He asked her why, now that her pain was under control, did she still want to die?

"You stupid man," she replied. "You stupid, stupid man."

Sixty-Seven

I have my mother's eyes they say. They are blue like hers, but they see things differently. I need glasses, but her eyesight was perfect. "There's nothing wrong with her eyes," her doctor told me when we discussed why she was losing her ability to read.

"I can read," she told me. "I just don't want to."

My dad viewed the world through trifocals and read about places that he would never go. I still remember the funeral director taking the glasses off his face and placing them in the casket before he closed the lid.

His eyes were hazel.

O

Sixty-Eight

It seems like only yesterday she was pushing him in his stroller careful not to wake him up. Seeing him push his motorcycle down the driveway so he wouldn't wake her up made her smile. She remembered him and his friends trying to creep up the stairs after coming in late whispering, "Dude — shhh!"

She was so tuned into him that as an infant she could hear him shift in his crib from the next room.

Still, one day she would be reading in the house and he would fall from the roof to his death silent as a leaf.

○

Sixty-Nine

The crazy hot yoga class is difficult. I find that I am re-energized when I see the youngsters around me begin to flail. The guys usually go down first; they just don't have the same mental toughness as women. I'm older than most of these kids' parents. I like to show them how it's done old school. That is, I like for them to see that there are certain times when their youth and beauty are of little use and for once I—paunchy, middle-aged broad who's learned how to take it in any number of ways—am the ideal.

○

Seventy

I called my mother as I was taking clothes out of the dryer.

"Why are you using a dryer in the summertime?" she asked. "You should hang your clothes outside."

"I live in an apartment," I replied.

"I was your age when we bought this house," she said.

"With all the money you saved from hanging out your clothes?"

"With frugality, my girl. You'll see."

"See what?" was what I refrained from asking. I knew better. Later, I strung clothesline like cat's cradle around the fire escape.

"What are you doing?" my roommate asked.

"Saving for a house," I said.

Seventy-One

Toddler life has an operatic quality. There's obvious drama, but there's also a lot of singing. Singing about dogs named Bingo and bus wheels, but also the putting on of shoes and eating three more bites of dinner. And, of course, poopies.

Poopies should not be confused with bowel movements. Bowel movements are adult activities that occur alone with *The New Yorker* after a second cup of coffee. Poopies are magical bodily functions. They are extravagant and public celebrations; wonderful whether performed by the child or a goat in a petting zoo.

Poopies are life; everything else is just shit.

Seventy-Two

Tough guys want Mary. They clamor for my attention and follow me everywhere. They want to talk. They want to make deals. They bargain with me, offering me all kinds of things—money and cars, anything I want. First, two make me an offer. Then three. Then more than I can count. It is ceaseless.

"No," I tell them. "No." They won't listen. I say: "No, no, no."

"Mary, Mary," they say. "We want Mary. Let us have Mary. We'll give you anything you want. Just let us have Mary."

"No," I say.

Tough guys want Mary.

But she's mine.

Seventy-Three

While on the phone with me my mother simply stopped talking and just put the phone down. I could hear her television and I could hear her adjusting herself in her wheelchair. We were still connected and I knew she was still there. What she couldn't hear, apparently, was me saying, "Mom? Mom! Hello! Mom! Hello, Mom!" But she had forgotten why the phone was against her ear. She had forgotten that phones were for talking, forgotten that she was on the phone with me, forgotten me, forgotten talking.

All I could say was hello. She had forgotten even goodbye.

Seventy-Four

Oh, life in the Bay Area was good! He loved living there with its abundance of natural beauty. The beach, the parks, and the weather all provided so many opportunities to explore and try new things.

He especially enjoyed the many free outdoor fairs and festivals that happened throughout the year. These events attracted large and varied crowds of all different sorts of people that he would never encounter otherwise.

He could sample different cultures, music, and food, but best of all, they offered chances to get really, really close, rub up against strangers, and touch them in inappropriate places.

Seventy-Five

When the men launched into weepy Irish songs and were emptying the bottles they'd brought, the women would sip Miller High Life to sober up so that they could drive them home. Once outside, the winter night air would finish reviving them. They would pour their men into the cars, get behind the wheel, and take them home. No one ever got killed and as far as I know no one ever got stopped. The women appeared sober and steady enough to perform surgery.

When called to action—crying child, blood, whatever—these women could sober up in a heartbeat.

O

Seventy-Six

This car is hell on tires and burns oil like a wok, but it can haul everything I own. It doesn't matter what kind of mileage you get when you don't drive very far. In fact, if someone doesn't tell me to move, I don't drive at all most days.

It's not bad out here. People don't mind my dogs and they don't care one way or the other about me so it's all just fine.

Had I known all along that it wasn't going to be so bad, I wouldn't have fought so hard to prevent it from happening.

○

Seventy-Seven

My father bought tie and handkerchief sets from the dry cleaners for a buck. He was almost buried in one of them until I found his shamrock tie just in time. Laid out, he looked a little like Milton Berle, which made the shamrock tie seem ironic. Perhaps a dry cleaner's set would have been the better choice.

At the wake a woman grabbed my mother's hands and exclaimed, "What a wonderful life you had together! How lucky you were to have found each other."

My mother squeezed the woman's hands and smiled at her. "Go fuck yourself," she said.

O

Seventy-Eight

When I finally broke up with my girlfriend for good, she thought it was because of her kid and I let her think that because it was partially true. The kid isn't a kid any more—he's twenty-two—and I've grown really fond of him. I've watched him mature and grow from a sullen punk to a thoughtful young man and I'm impressed with the people he hangs around with. He's accomplished, he's athletic, he's funny.

The truth is I've watched him march along with his life while his mother desperately lives through his experiences.

I should start dating him.

Seventy-Nine

My mother lied about her height. It was easy to disprove, but as far as I know, no one ever challenged her on it.

She claimed to be two inches taller than she was and people believed her, I think, because she gave the impression of being tall.

She would admit her actual age in a heartbeat because she loved being told she looked much younger. Her weight was a well-guarded secret. But her height was a complete fabrication she took to her grave.

Perhaps this overt lie was her way of shielding from scrutiny all the others she told.

Eighty

There was a place in London's Soho that my boyfriend called "Cunt Corner" because everything you could see was a solicitation for sex. The area was very English; its prurient material was coupled with a British attitude that nothing was untoward.

Once he had shown me the place, I would find myself wandering there even though it was off my path. I was deeply curious—and curious about being curious.

My boyfriend got worried. Our relationship was in trouble. He was becoming increasingly needy, fretful that we were breaking up.

He was a great boyfriend. I was just a lesbian.

Eighty-One

A woman in a rowboat on a lake wants to dangle her feet in the water, but the water is like glass—it might, in fact, be glass—and she is afraid to break its surface.

She has a basket of sandwiches wrapped in bright paper. Every time she opens a sandwich, it turns into a butterfly and flies away.

After she rows ashore a man asks her for food. She points to the basket. He looks in it, but finds only empty wrappers.

"How do you stay so thin?" he marvels, and pushes her boat back into the water.

Eighty-Two

The argument was over from my perspective. I'd won but I could tell by the furious knitting of his eyebrows that he was only ceding this round while he created his rebuttal in his head, mentally scratching out words, inserting others.

A sly smile played across his lips and I could tell he had thought of something really good to say, something that was really going to get me. He would extract his revenge and prevail.

"Once you finish fixing my wagon, could you take a look at the dishwasher?"

Thwarted, he was crestfallen.

Hey, it's marriage not the UN.

Eighty-Three

My mother once gave me a home permanent. I wouldn't go to school the next day and my mother actually let me stay home. Even she thought the results were hideous.

She told me that the perm would "relax." My hair looked like an electrocuted poodle; "relax" seemed like the wrong word.

Years later as I sat on the toilet destroying dozens of tampons trying to insert one for the first time, my mother stood outside the door telling me to "relax."

I felt like I was shoving an axe handle up my vagina. "Relax" was *really* the wrong word.

O

Eighty-Four

Change affects people in different ways. Me, I like variety. Not knowing what's going to happen one minute to the next is exhilarating.

But my sister is a whole other story. She needs everything just so. It's important to her to know what's coming and what to expect. She'd no sooner change laundry soap brands than cut off her arm. Of course, they say it's all because of Roy and what he did and the shock.

Poor Ellen, they blame it all on Roy and "that Vietnamese girl," but really, she never got over when they changed Darrins on *Bewitched*.

Eighty-Five

She was sitting beside me naked on a bench in the women's locker room. She was white like talc and smelled faintly of Aqua Net and urine.

"My best friend is deaf," she told me. "She went to deaf school and learned sign language. She reads lips, too, but when I'm with her I am always careful about what I do with my hands. I wouldn't want to say something by accident that would offend or upset her—she's my best friend after all."

"What do you talk about?" I asked.

"Oh, everything," she said. "She's such a great listener."

O

Eighty-Six

As a manager, I participated in disaster planning meetings. It seemed to me that we needn't plan for disasters. They happened with alarming frequency.

Who were we kidding? We couldn't even get the fat guy to stop eating other people's lunches. In a real disaster, a true emergency, we wouldn't be able to find our butts with both hands.

Nevertheless, we muddled through documenting methods for notifying staff, safety, system redundancies, etcetera, after a "real" catastrophe struck.

These documents are most likely useless—although they might have kept some bad managers busy enough to prevent making a few stupid decisions.

Eighty-Seven

She wears her hair the same way she did when her skin finally cleared up when she was twenty-two. The acne scars still show, as do her roots — now wintry gray instead of mousy brown. Her monthly ash blonde dye job now happens every eight weeks. Maybe.

The shag and the ash blonde were acquired when everyone wanted to be Judy Carne or Goldie Hawn. With the cut and the color, she chose a little of both.

She has kept it up because she thinks it makes her look young, mistaking a choice made in her youth for youth itself.

Eighty-Eight

They get two weeks off at Christmas out here. The kids all view it as their birthright not coming from a place where the school year had to accommodate snow days and only one miserly week would be granted at the holidays.

For me, there was an inordinate amount of church during the holidays as Christmas and New Year's were both holy days of obligation and Sunday continued to be Sunday, vacation or no.

The week went fast like runners on a well-waxed sled.

Sun on snow can blind you; you only see clearly many years later in your mind.

Eighty-Nine

She asked if I minded and I kept telling her that I didn't.

"You're sure you don't mind," she'd say.

"Yes, I'm sure," I'd reply.

Repeatedly, when she'd ask me, "You're absolutely sure that you don't mind?" I'd say: "I'm absolutely sure."

Eventually, I began thinking, "Should I mind? Am I being a fool? What am I getting myself into?" Yet, I continued to assure her that I didn't mind.

She finally stopped asking, but by the time she left I had memorized all her emergency numbers.

Once alone, I chained the door, checking it several times throughout the night.

Ninety

He wore a necktie for important meetings. No one wore ties at his office, but he believed that wearing one showed his supervisors that he was sincere and professional.

His coworkers considered him ridiculous for wearing a tie. Some even felt that the tie indicated contempt for them. Many made fun of him and thought the tie was silly—like something your mother would make you do on picture day at school.

In fact, his mother had made him wear a tie to school on picture day. She told him it made him stand out.

His supervisors didn't even notice.

Ninety-One

She knew he'd want to have sex before the epi-siotomy stitches had dissolved. He would be on top of her grunting with the baby beside them crying and the kids carrying on somewhere else in the house. When she was little playing with her dolls she never thought much about where babies came from. She imagined that babies and daddies came from a store and you got to pick them out.

"Someone needs to make a slobbering, unshav-en husband doll," she thought. "And a fat, sleep-de-prived wife to go beneath him. Scare a girl celibate faster than a loaded diaper."

O

Ninety-Two

She had taken to wearing small clip-on hairpieces. She had several of them in different colors and would clip them onto various places in her hair. Sometimes she used one, sometimes many. It would look as if she had exotic small animals burrowing on her head.

This habit became deeply troubling to many who knew her.

"It looks...well, I don't get it," one good friend said.

"Do you want people to think that you're crazy?" her sister asked.

She didn't care. Pointing out other people's insecurities to them was her mission in life.

And she was very good at it.

○

Ninety-Three

Michael has long been on a restricted diet. He can't eat dairy, salt, or much of anything good. He brings me inedible cookies his wife bakes for him.

"These aren't too bad," he says as he puts one on a napkin and slides it over.

He's not aware that his taste buds have grown used to his wife's loving efforts, but mine have not nor will I ever let them.

"Thanks," I say. "I'll make a cup of tea." And I do, and drink it waiting for the right moment to slip the cookie into the trash.

Poor sweet man.

O

Ninety-Four

Seeing her breasts through that blouse — that blouse! — with her big jewelry and her big *her*, I'm suddenly a kid on a Saturday watching Dominic wrap my family's meat order at Top Dollar. He's making a bundle of ground chuck and roast beef and pork chops that my mother will smother in Shake 'n Bake until this little piggy begs to be let off at the next stop.

Meanwhile I'm staring at the deli meat counter and, *marone*, the mortadella and bologna are flaunting themselves at me behind chrome and glass.

When Wonder Bras wonder what do they wonder about?

Ninety-Five

My mother was away on one of her "stays."

One night I woke to hear rhythmic creaking noises. I summoned my courage to go look.

It was my Dad.

His back was to me and I could see his stubby hairy legs sticking out from below my mother's Sunday coat. He had on the hat she wore to church. As I watched him, he swayed into a slow foxtrot.

I crawled soundlessly back to bed. There was never a time I could ask him about that night and there has never been a time when I have not wanted to.

Ninety-Six

Of course I have fantasies. Everyone does, right? It's a normal and predictable part of transference. Healthy.

Initially, the fantasies would pop into my mind fully formed. Now, I'm able to control the scenarios. I imagine us being best friends, hanging out, doing things. I imagine us being girlfriends and doing, well, other things. Those times, depending on whether I'm channeling my inner child, imaginary friend or evil twin, I mentally dress her up. Sometimes she's a nun, Xena, Annie Oakley, an airline stewardess circa 1963, or maybe just in high heels and handcuffs.

Did I say that out loud?

Ninety-Seven

Jackie's mother's dinner every night was the free appetizers at the bar near her trailer park.

Her mother would buy a dollar glass of Chablis and make her way through the Swedish meatballs and Buffalo wings. After thirty-three years of clerical work, raising three kids alone, she could barely afford her trailer much less buy food.

"Your father didn't just leave me," she said. "He stripped me bare."

We were all working our way through school at the time, facing years of student loans, and soon, our own confrontations with disappointment.

"She never understood nutrition," was all Jackie could say.

Ninety-Eight

All morning a bird flew against my window. Drunk on pyracantha berries, he mistook his reflection for a competing male. Or he was a crazy bird. Who is to say there isn't mental illness in the animal world? He might have been trying to kill himself. Perhaps he had just murdered his entire family and now was trying to do himself in. Perhaps he was despondent over the condition of the world and his inability to do anything about it. "What can I do? I'm just one bird," he might have thought.

But probably it was that pyracantha berries thing.

Ninety-Nine

It was snowing and blowing crazy hard—sideways almost. The weather didn't bother the deer much; he stepped steadily to reach the shelter of a thicket fifty feet away. It bothered the car a great deal; it had been surging and skidding for miles.

When they faced each other, the car panicked and stalled while the deer in three quick springs entered the safety of the woods where he went on to rut and sire many offspring.

The car barely made it back to its garage and when it got there, bled out from a cracked master cylinder and died.

O

One Hundred

At the ocean's edge, I imagined I saw a bed sheet just below the waves breaking at the shore. The sheet, submerged twisted confusion, seemed curiously free, liberated from its burden of having others' dreams and love occur upon it. I sometimes think I dream of swimming. In these dreams I think I have I am just below the surface in a submerged twisted confusion, but curiously free. Perhaps in these dreams I want to have I am liberated from all of my own expectations and lust and can relax finally as the darkness breaks so brightly all around me.

Acknowledgments

Thank you to judge Jacob M. Appel for selecting my work for the Michael Rubin Book Award. Other entrants for this award included some of my favorite writers. I am grateful and humbled.

Thank you to Toni Mirosevich and Chanan Tigay for their kind words and generosity.

A writer couldn't hope for better editors and partners than Shadia Savo and Ryan Nash. You've both been so much fun to work with and have treated my work with exquisite care.

Thank you Fourteen Hills Press for publishing my little book.

My dear and talented friend Cathy Ryan lent the artwork for the cover of this book. Thank you, Cathy.

Thank you to my Other Jane who knows how meaningful numbers are to me.

Thank you to early readers Don Lloyd, Prudy Kohler, Loren Partridge, and Mary Swope.

I am grateful to my family—real and imagined, alive and dead. You have influenced my work in strange and wonderful ways.

I love the MA/MFA Creative Writing Program at San Francisco State University and everyone in it.

And, finally, thanks to my sweet wife Mary—my harshest critic and fiercest advocate—for joining me on this intrepid journey. Girl, we're just getting started.

About the Author

Jane McDermott was born and raised in Boston, Massachusetts. She has a BFA in filmmaking from the San Francisco Art Institute, had a nearly thirty-year career in marketing/marketing communications, and is a MFA candidate in creative writing at San Francisco State University. Her work has appeared in the anthologies *How Running Changed My Life: True Stories of the Power of Running* (Breakaway Books, NY, 2002) and *Knit Lit the Third: We Spin More Yarns* (Three Rivers Press, NY, 2005), as well as the journals *The Rambler, Reunion: The Dallas Review,* and SFSU's own *Transfer Magazine.* She has been a featured reader at Writing without Walls, The Hazel Reading Series, Bay Area Generations, and Beast Crawl. This is her first book.

Jane lives in Oakland, California, with her wife and assorted cats, chickens, and bees. She tries to find time to be grateful every day.